Nidoran's New Friend

#7

Pokémon junior™

There are more books about Pokémon for younger readers.

COLLECT THEM ALL!

#1 Surf's Up, Pikachu!

#2 Meowth, the Big Mouth

#3 Save Our Squirtle!

#4 Bulbasaur's Bad Day

#5 Two of a Kind

#6 Raichu Shows Off

#7 Nidoran's New Friend

COMING SOON!

#8 A Pokémon Snow-down

Nidoran's New Friend

#7 Pokémon junior™

Adapted by Gregg Sacon

SCHOLASTIC INC.
New York Toronto London Auckland Sydney
Mexico City New Delhi Hong Kong

ISBN 0-439-20096-2

24 23 22 21 20 19 18 17 16 15 8 9/9 0 1 2/0

Printed in the U.S.A.

First Scholastic printing, October 2000

CHAPTER ONE

The Missing Nidoran

Pikachu and Ash Ketchum were walking through a small town. The Pokémon and its trainer were on a quest. Ash wanted to become the world's greatest Pokémon trainer. And Pikachu wanted to help.

"This town sure is quiet," said

Tracey. Tracey was one of Ash's good friends. Tracey liked to watch Pokémon and draw them.

"It is small," said Ash, "but it is a nice town."

"My canteen is empty," Misty said. Misty and her tiny Pokémon, Togepi, always went with Ash and Pikachu on their adventures.

"Really?" Ash said. "Maybe we can find a water fountain."

Just then, the friends heard a voice cry out.

"Maria! Where are you?" the voice said.

Pikachu spun around. It was a pretty girl in a pink dress. Her name was Emily.

"Have you seen Maria, my Nidoran Pokémon?" she asked. "She is blue and has big ears. She is so cute."

Ash pulled out Dexter, his Pokédex. Dexter knew everything about Pokémon.

"Nidoran, male," Dexter said.

"Wait!" said

Emily.

"Maria is a girl Nidoran."

"Nidoran, female," Dexter said. "Smaller than the male. Its Poison Pin is very powerful."

"Wow," Misty said. "The male and female look different."

"I cannot take my eyes off Maria," Emily said, "or she will run away."

"Really?" asked Ash. "We will help you look for her."

They all set out to find Maria.

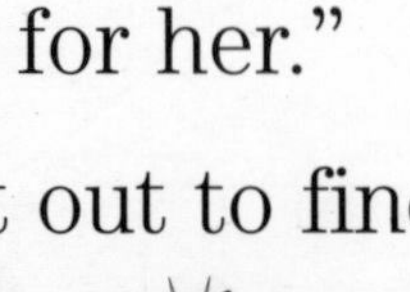

CHAPTER TWO

The Search Is On!

"Here, girl Nidoran! Where are you?" Ash yelled.

"Ash!" said Misty. "Call her by her name!"

"Oh, yeah," said Ash. "Maria! Maria!"

It was later that day. They still had not found Emily's Nidoran.

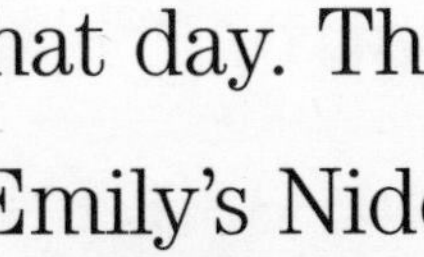

Then Pikachu heard a voice. "Where are you, Tony?" the voice said. It was a boy in a blue shirt. His name was Ralph.

"Have you seen Tony?" Ralph said. "He is my Nidoran Pokémon."

"Pika pika?" wondered Pikachu. *Another Nidoran?*

"Tony is a boy Nidoran," Ralph said. "He is so cool. But he always runs away."

"Nidoran, male," Dexter said. "Its Horn Attack and Poison Sting are very strong."

Pikachu, Ash, and Misty were

confused. Now there were two Nidoran missing!

Just then, Tracey and Emily came running up the street.

"Did you find Maria?" Ash said.

"Not yet," said Tracey.

Then Pikachu and its friends got a surprise. When Ralph and Emily saw each other, they began screaming.

"Where are you hiding Tony?" Ralph shouted.

"You stole Maria!" yelled Emily.

Ralph and Emily picked up sticks. They began to fight!

Pikachu frowned. It did not like fighting.

"Please stop that!" said Misty.

Then Tracey's Pokémon Marill appeared. Marill had special hearing. It could track down anything!

"Marill marill!" it told them. *I found the Nidoran!*

Ralph and Emily dashed away.

CHAPTER THREE

The Two Nidoran

Ralph and Emily ran into a pretty garden. The two Nidoran were playing together. The boy Nidoran, Tony, looked like a pink dinosaur. The girl, Maria, was as blue as the sky.

"Tony!" cried Ralph.

"Maria!" cried Emily.

The two Nidoran were bumping their noses together.

"Look how happy they are," said Misty.

Tony picked a flower from a bush. He gave the flower to Maria. She smiled at him.

"*Pika pi,*" thought Pikachu.

They are such good friends!

But Ralph and Emily were angry. They did not like their Pokémon playing together.

"I do not want you seeing that Nidoran again," Emily said. She grabbed Maria and stomped away.

"That thing is not fit for you," said Ralph. He picked up Tony and stormed away, too.

The Nidoran sadly waved good-bye.

"They were so happy!" Ash said.

"*Pika pika,*" Pikachu cried.

They were in love!

Later that day, Pikachu and its friends were eating in a diner. They told the cook about what happened with the two Nidoran.

"Do you know Ralph and Emily?" Tracey asked.

"Everyone knows them," the cook replied. "They love Pokémon. But they have been fighting with each other since they were children. They always enter Pokémon contests, and it's a huge battle to decide which one of them wins.

"This year, they both entered their Nidoran. It was a tie

between them. When their Nidoran met, they fell in love. But because their trainers do not like each other, their Pokémon can never be together."

"I feel sorry for those poor Nidoran," said Misty.

"*Pika,*" said Pikachu. *Me, too.*

CHAPTER FOUR

Broken Hearts

That evening, Pikachu and its friends walked through town.

"Those poor Nidoran," Misty said. "They love each other. But their trainers keep fighting."

"Look!" said Ash. "There goes one now!"

Sure enough, the boy Nidoran,

Tony, was hopping across the street!

They all followed him to a big house and hid behind a bush. Pikachu could see Tony going up to the house.

"*Nidoran!*" he cried. He was looking up to the second floor.

"*Nidoran!*" came a voice from above. It was the girl Nidoran, Maria. She was on the balcony.

"What are they doing?" Ash wondered.

"They are saying how much they like each other," said Misty.

Suddenly, Emily appeared on the balcony. And she was not happy to see Tony.

"Stop bugging Maria!" she said. She grabbed a pail of water.

"Pika-chuuuuu!" Pikachu cried. *Look out, Tony!*

But it was too late! Emily had

thrown the water over the ledge.

Splash! Tony was soaked!

Emily picked up Maria. She stormed

inside the house.

Just then, Ralph came along.

"Tony!" he cried. "Look what Emily did to you!"

Ralph ran to Tony and dried him off. The Nidoran Pokémon was sad. He could see Maria inside the house. He wanted to be with her.

“This is what happens when you leave home without me,” Ralph said. Ralph and Tony walked down a short path. It led to Ralph’s house — right next door.

“We have to help those Nidoran,” Misty said.

“Pikaaa,” thought Pikachu. *It will not be easy.*

Across the street, a teenage boy and girl were hiding behind a tree. They were watching Tony and Maria, too.

It was Team Rocket, Pikachu and Ash's worst enemies!

"First we will steal the Nidoran," said James.

"And then we will bring them to the boss," said Jessie.

Meowth laughed. Meowth was Team Rocket's Pokémon. It looked like a kitten. But it liked to fight.

"We are lucky," Meowth said happily. "Two Nidoran make a great gift set!"

CHAPTER FIVE

Misty's Plan

"What are you doing?" Ash said.

"I am writing letters to Ralph and Emily," said Misty. "I am pretending they wrote each other the letters. I want to help them make up. Then they will let their Nidoran be together."

Pikachu and its friends were at

the Pokémon Center. It had been a long day. Now it was late, and Pikachu was sleepy.

"What do the letters say?" Ash said.

"I am sorry I was mean to you, Ralph," read Misty. "I really liked you the whole time. Love, Emily."

Pikachu knew what Misty was up to. She was trying to trick Ralph and Emily into liking each other!

"Are you sure you should do this, Misty?" Ash asked.

"Positive," she said.

"*Pika,*" Pikachu whispered. *I hope this works!*

Meanwhile, Jessie and James were hiding below Emily's window.

"We will trick the Nidoran into coming with us," James said. "They care about each other. So they will want to be together."

Jessie looked up at Emily's house. "Meowth, you go steal those lovers!" she ordered.

"Aye aye, sir!" said Meowth.

CHAPTER SIX

Watch Out, Maria!

Emily was fast asleep in her bed. Maria was lying in a basket nearby, covered with blankets. But she was awake.

"I have great news," a voice said. "You can finally be happy."

Maria looked out the window. It was Meowth.

“Come with me,” said Meowth. “And you and Tony can be together.”

Maria climbed from her basket. She walked to the window. That was exactly what Meowth wanted!

Below the window, Jessie and James were waiting.

“First, the Nidoran will be married,” Jessie said. “Then we will pretend we are taking them

on their honeymoon. But we will really take them to the boss."

Just then, Meowth returned. "Maria would not come out. She said Pokémon cannot disobey their trainers."

"But they are in love!" said Jessie. "Nothing should stand in their way!"

Jessie and James were mad. Their plan had failed.

"Now what do we do?" James asked.

Jessie laughed a mean laugh. "We take them by force."

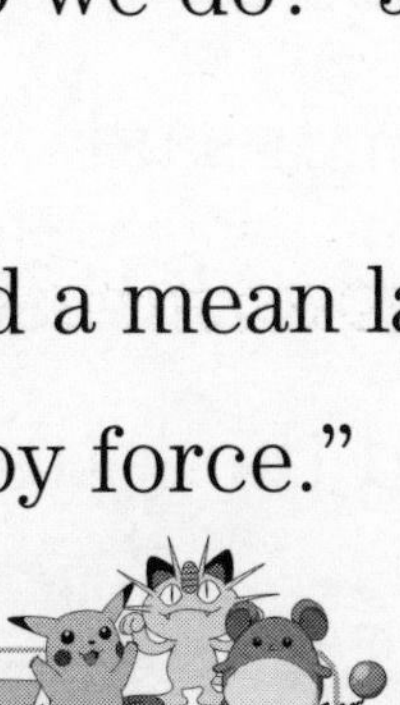

CHAPTER SEVEN

A Wedding?

The next morning, Pikachu and his friends stood in the garden. They were waiting for Ralph and Emily.

"Are you sure they will come, Misty?" Ash said.

"I think so," Misty said. "Once they read the letters I wrote."

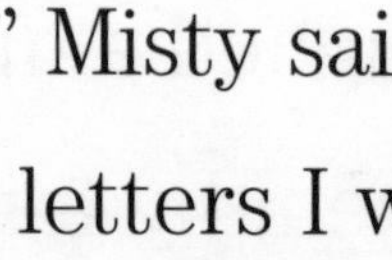

Misty was trying to trick Ralph and Emily into becoming friends. That way, their Nidoran could be together. She had sent flowers to Emily, pretending they were from Ralph. And she had sent a model airplane to Ralph, pretending it was from Emily.

"Wait!" Tracey whispered. "Here they come!"

Ralph and Emily walked into the garden. Ralph had his airplane. And Emily had her flowers.

"Why did you send me that

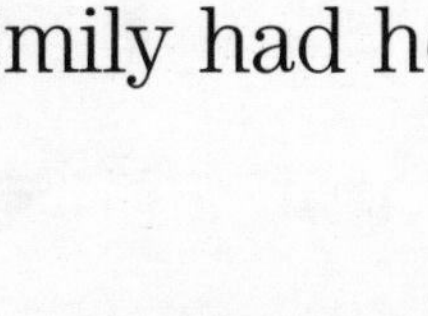

stupid letter?" Ralph and Emily asked at the same time.

The two trainers stared at each other. "Wait a minute. You —" they cried at the same time.

"I hate model airplanes!" Ralph yelled.

"I bet you knew I am allergic to flowers!" Emily screamed.

Ralph and Emily began fighting. Misty looked sad. Her plan had not worked.

"I guess I still have some things to learn about love," she said.

"*Pika pi,*" thought Pikachu. *Me, too.*

Then a strange thing happened. Wedding music filled the air!

Pikachu turned around. A bride and groom were walking into the garden.

"Look," Misty said. "A wedding!"

"Today is our special day," the bride said.

"And we will celebrate by taking these Nidoran as presents!" said the groom.

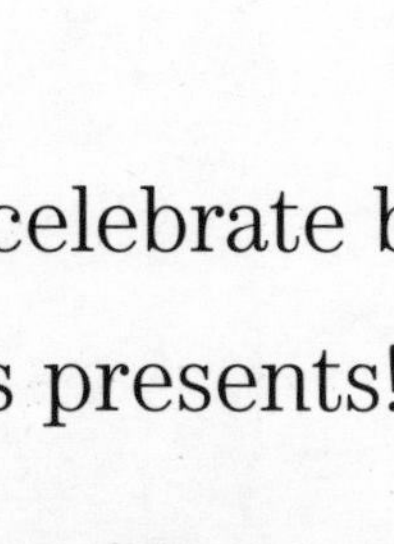

The bride grabbed Tony. The groom grabbed Maria. They threw the Nidoran into metal cages.

"Pikachu!" Ash said. "We have to save them!"

Pikachu and Ash ran as fast as they could. But the bride and groom had disappeared!

"Where did they go?" Ash wondered.

CHAPTER EIGHT

The Giant Balloon

"Pika pi," said Pikachu. *There they are! Up in the sky!*

The bride and groom were in a giant hot air balloon. It was shaped like Meowth. There were empty cans tied to the bottom.

It was Team Rocket!

"Good-bye!" James yelled. "And

thanks for these Nidoran!"

"Do not worry," Ash told Ralph and Emily. "We will get your Nidoran back."

"But how?" Emily said.

Suddenly, Pikachu jumped up and down! *"Pikachu! Pika!"* There was a trail of cans across the ground. They had fallen off the balloon. They could follow the cans to Team Rocket!

Ash smiled at his Pokémon. "Great idea, Pikachu!" he said.

CHAPTER NINE

Fighting for Love

On the other end of town, Team Rocket was celebrating.

"We did it!" James said.

Then a sound made them turn. *Clang!* Ash kicked an empty can toward Team Rocket.

"How did you find us?" Jessie grumbled.

"We followed the cans you left behind," said Ash.

Tony and Maria leaped from their cages.

"You will not get away!" said Jessie. "Go, Arbok!"

Arbok flew out of Jessie's Poké Ball. It looked like a big snake.

"Look out, Tony!" shouted Ash.

Arbok tackled the little Nidoran.

"Fight back!" said Ralph.

Tony and Maria flew at Arbok.

Tony attacked with his horn. Maria slammed Arbok with a Tail Whip.

"Arbok!" Arbok roared as it tumbled onto its back.

"Go, Victreebel!" said James.

With a roar, the Plant Pokémon flew through the air and tackled Jessie!

"Not me, them!" yelled Jessie.

"Pikachu!" shouted Pikachu. *Now is your chance!*

Tony and Maria ran at Arbok. They began to battle. First, the Nidoran were winning. Then Arbok was winning. Then Tony

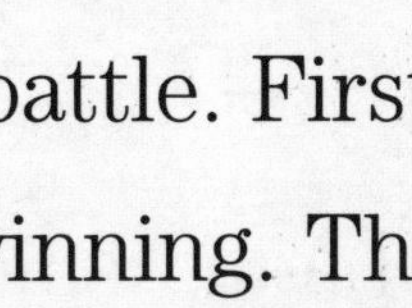

dropped Arbok with an Energy Focus Attack.

"Those Nidoran are pretty good," Ash said.

"Pika!" said Pikachu. *Yeah!*

"Sleep Powder, Victreebel!" called James. "Arbok, Bite!"

Victreebel and Arbok were bigger than Tony and Maria. But the Nidoran were better fighters.

"Tony is fighting for Maria," Ralph realized.

"Maria is fighting because she loves Tony," said Emily slowly.

Tony hammered Arbok with his Fury Swipes. Arbok fainted. At the same time, Maria blasted Victreebel with a Double Kick.

"*Pika pika!*" yelled Pikachu. *They did it!*

Tony and Maria were free — but not for long!

Suddenly, Pikachu heard a loud noise. Team Rocket was escaping in the hot air balloon. Meowth had turned on a big vacuum. It was pulling Tony and Maria off the ground. They were being sucked through the air!

Soon they would be inside Team Rocket's balloon!

CHAPTER TEN

Together at Last!

Ash turned to his Pokémon. "Pikachu!" he said. "Help us out."

"Pik-a-chuuuuu!" Pikachu blasted the balloon with electricity! The force was so strong, Meowth dropped the vacuum.

"Way to go, Pikachu!" cried Ash.

"Go, Staryu!" ordered Misty.

Staryu attacked the balloon. Its sharp points burst the balloon and

sent it zooming through the air.

"Looks like Team Rocket is blasting off again!" cried Jessie.

"Serves you right," said Misty. "That is what happens when you mess with true love!"

Ralph and Emily hugged their Nidoran.

"What do you say?" Misty

asked. “Are you two ready to let your Nidoran be together?”

“I would like that,” Emily said. “But I could never give Maria away.”

“And I could never part with Tony,” said Ralph.

“Maybe you do not have to,” Tracey said. “You live next door to each other. You should build a little home for your Nidoran, between your houses. Then you can watch over them together.”

Ralph and Emily liked the idea. They smiled at each other for the very first time ever.

"So it is decided!" Misty said. "Now your Nidoran will always be together. And so will you!"

This made Tony and Maria very happy. They rubbed their noses together. Then something wonderful happened! The Nidoran began to grow. Maria turned darker blue. Her horns became

bigger. Tony's ears and teeth grew. Now they were Nidorino and Nidorina!

"The Nidoran evolved!" Misty shouted. "It is like a fairy tale."

Then Ralph and Emily gathered up their Nidoran and waved good-bye.

"I am so happy for those Nidoran!" Misty said.

"I wonder what they will do now," said Ash.

"*Pika pi,*" smiled Pikachu.

They will live happily ever after.

Snowed In!

Pokémon junior™

Chapter Book #8:

A Pokémon Snow-down

Ash and Pikachu are hiking through the mountains with Misty and Brock. But when a big blizzard strikes, Ash and Pikachu get lost in the blinding storm. Now the two friends are cold and lost—and it's almost dark. Can Ash, Pikachu, Bulbasaur, Squirtle, Charmander, and Pidgetto survive the freezing night on their own?

Coming soon to a bookstore near you!

Visit us at www.scholastic.com

SCHOLASTIC

POKJPooc